A GOOD TRADE

Alma Fullerton

Illustrations by Karen Patkau

pajamapress

First published in the United States in 2013
Text copyright © Alma Fullerton
Illustration copyright © Karen Patkau
This edition copyright © 2012 Pajama Press

10 9 8 7 6 5 4 3 2

Canada Council   Conseil des arts
for the Arts   du Canada

OA ONTARIO ARTS COUNCIL
    CONSEIL DES ARTS DE L'ONTARIO

The publisher gratefully acknowledges the support of the Canada Council for the Arts and the Ontario
Arts Council for its publishing program. We acknowledge the financial support of the Government of
Canada through the Canada Book Fund (CBF) for our publishing activities.

Library and Archives Canada Cataloguing in Publication

Fullerton, Alma

    A good trade / Alma Fullerton ; illustrated by Karen Patkau.

ISBN 978-0-9869495-9-3

    I. Patkau, Karen II. Title.

PS8611.U45G66 2012   jC813'.6   C2012-904355-9

Publisher Cataloging-in-Publication Data (U.S.)

Fullerton, Alma, 1969- .
    A good trade / Alma Fullerton ; illustrated by Karen
Patkau.
[   ] p. : col. ill. ;   cm.
Summary: Every day Kato trudges barefoot past fields and soldiers on the long, hot road to his Ugandan
village well. When an aid worker brings a life-changing gift of shoes for all the village children, Kato find
something to give her in return: one small piece of beauty in a war-torn land
ISBN-13: 978-0-9869495-9-3
1. Ugandan children – Juvenile fiction.   2. Children and war – Uganda – Juvenile fiction.   3. Poverty –
Uganda – Juvenile fiction.   I. Patkau, Karen, 1951 - .   II. Title.
[E] dc23   PZ7.F8554Go   2012

Manufactured by Friesens in Altona, Manitoba, Canada in April 2013.

Pajama Press Inc.
469 Richmond St E, Toronto Ontario, Canada
www.pajamapress.ca

Distributed in the U.S. by **Orca Book Publishers**
PO Box 468 Custer, WA, 98240-0468, USA

To Claude
— Alma Fullerton

To Alvan Small
— Karen Patkau

In a small Ugandan garden,
a single poppy blooms
white in a sea of green.

On a mat inside his hut,
Kato wakes
at the break of dawn.

Across his sleeping village,

Kato skips,

swinging two empty jerry cans.

Beyond the village gate,

Kato races

through the grass

and down a rut-filled hill.

Along a matted trail,
Kato treks past cattle-spotted fields
guarded by soldiers.

At the borehole,
Kato fills his jerry cans
with a day's supply of water,
splashing it onto his dusty feet.

Struggling up the hill,
Kato hauls his load—

one on his head
and one in his hand—

then pauses for a rest.

Near the village square,
Kato dawdles

as an aid worker's truck
rumbles to a halt,
and he peeks inside.

Past his waking neighbors,
Kato hurries,
the water sloshing
inside the jerry cans.

Rushing through his chores,

Kato runs to the garden

and stops

when he spies

the single white poppy.

Tenderly, he kneels
to pick it.

Between bouncy children,
Kato weaves, cradling the poppy,
careful not to crush it.

First in line,

Kato gives his poppy to a woman,

who makes a good trade.

In his small Ugandan village,

Kato dances with friends,

wearing

his brand—new shoes.